CREATURE FEATURES

USA TODAY BESTSELLING AUTHOR

N GRAY

VINCI
BOOKS

"Whoever fights monsters should see to it that in the process he does not become a monster.
And if you gaze long enough into an abyss, the abyss will gaze back into you."

— *Friedrich Nietzsche*

Vinci Books

vinci-books.com

Published by Vinci Books Ltd in 2026

1

The EU GPSR authorised representative is Logos Europe, 9 rue Nicolas
Poussion, 17000 La Rochelle, France
contact@logoseurope.eu

By N Gray

Shifter Days, Vampire Nights & Demons in Between

Twisted

Lady Hawk and Her Mountain Man

Hidden Shifter

Wolf

Wolf Retreat

Night Hunter

The Fixer

Kai

Lee

Flynn

Jude

More from N Gray writing as Natalie Michaels

Steve Campbell Psychological Suspense Thrillers

The Last Girl

The Bone Forest

The White Dahlia

I See You

Death in the City

More from N Gray writing as SD Syns

The Diaries

Red Lace Diaries

www.ngraybooks.com

ONE

Dusty

Dr. Byrd's mustache was a little long and curled inside his mouth. Did food ever get caught on the wiry strands? How often did he trim it? Did he put any of those fancy oils or wax on it to keep it smooth? Would he allow Dusty to touch it?

Dr. Byrd lifted his hand and waved it in front of Dusty's face, bringing her out of her daydream.

"Hmm." She gazed into Dr. Byrd's brown eyes, giving him her full attention.

Dr. Byrd read from his notes. "You mentioned your dog attacked the man who delivered a package to your home. I asked how bad the bite was and if he's all right now?"

"Oh! Right."

That wasn't what really happened, that's just what she told Dr. Byrd.

Dusty shifted in the large chair. "The courier guy. Yes, I helped him. It was just a minor scratch, luckily nothing worth complaining to the police about."

Not really, it wasn't her dog; they didn't even own one.

The courier guy teased her sons, and he ended up with a large gash on his forearm. With an apology, many threats, and a bag full of money, she could sort out any *misunderstanding*. Last she heard, the man had moved to Mauritius and was living the rest of his days doing whatever he wanted while enjoying the sun—and their money.

Since that episode, Dusty had worried about her son's and how they needed to control themselves. That thought alone sent shivers down her spine.

Control.

They need *discipline*—that was more appropriate. But she new she couldn't blame them, they all shared the similar temper.

Dr. Byrd finished his therapy mumbo jumbo and mentioned homework she needed to do for her next session. Sigh! She wanted to roll her eyes, but he was watching her with his brown hawk eyes over glass frames. She still had too many sessions left with Dr. Byrd. She didn't know whether she had the strength to continue—the *restraint*. To experience such proximity to someone who smelled so delicious was testing her willpower to the fullest. Dusty needed to set a good example for her sons and wished she could snap her fingers and be back at the hospital already.

Dr. Byrd stopped talking, her cue to rise. He shook her hand, and she could smell his sour breath; she didn't think he flossed much, if at all. He had an excellent head of dark brown hair that looked soft like a baby's. She wanted to run her fingers through it, to feel how soft it was. His handshake was firm yet soft like his belly; he probably drank a beer or two after work. And, he wasn't very active—he sounded out of breath by the time they reach the door—it's almost too easy. Dusty wouldn't work too hard to catch him. Sweat trickled down Dusty's spine, and her beast wanted to explode out of her body and grab him. Her hands bunched into fists, she fought the temptation, the delicious meaty smell. She wished she could take a bite—just one tasty bite.

Dusty's dream shattered when the receptionist opened the door, and Dr. Byrd's next victim entered his office.

After Dusty's consultation with the psychologist, she stopped at the local grocery store for a few items. Two women were gossiping as she passed them and overheard that the Cravens had moved back to town. The news stopped Dusty in her tracks, and the two women stared at her—they knew she had been listening. Dusty grabbed the last of the items she needed and paid. It's been two years since they last saw the Cravens. Their two families shared bad blood between them, and she was unsure how the Cravens would make it right again—if at all. She needed to keep her sons away from their daughters. When little girls became women, boys turned into their destined animal.

Once home, Dusty packed away the items she bought from the grocery store, wiped down the kitchen counter, and went into her study across the hallway. Her office had one of the better views of the trees outside and displayed the mountain that surrounded them. Just as she settled behind her computer, the boys started stomping down the stairs like baby elephants. The fridge door opened. She had just cleaned the kitchen.

"If you make a mess, you tidy up!" she yelled from her office.

"Yes, Mom," they said in unison.

Dusty knew that sarcastic tone of theirs, rose from her desk, and quietly crossed the hallway to the kitchen. When she reached the doorjamb, she peeked around the corner but remained outside their line of sight. Her two sons were standing next to each other near the floating island where she usually prepared meals. Damian had his back to Dusty; he was a little taller and more masculine than Duke. They both had sandy brown hair; Duke's was untidy and a little longer around the ears, while Damian preferred to keep his short and neat. Dusty could see Duke's face and he rolled his eyes.

"Did you just roll your eyes at me?" she said into the passage so that her voice echoed throughout the house.

"How do you know?" Duke asked, glancing around.

Dusty giggled into her hands. "I am your mother and I know everything."

Damian punched Duke on the shoulder.

"Ouch! What did you do that for?" Duke cried.

"There is no way Mom can say that unless she saw you, you idiot." Damian punched him again.

"Mom! Tell Damian to stop it."

Dusty laughed and entered the kitchen. "Okay, stop it now, Damian. Hit your brother again, and I will ground you."

Duke stuck his tongue out at his brother.

"Duke, you aren't six."

Duke slithered his tongue back inside his mouth.

"What time are we catching dinner?" Damian stuffed a handful of last night's leftover meat in his mouth.

"Seven should be fine. It will be nice and dark out. The neighbors are coming up for the weekend, so we need to catch enough to last us till after they leave next week. We can't have their son see us again."

These were the neighbors who lived closest to Dusty's house. They came up often to spend weekends at their cabin, away from their city life. Dusty got on with them, and they called her before they arrived so she could unlock their cabin for the cleaning services. That way, Dusty knew when they were coming, and her family could prepare well in advance.

Duke cowered back into the fridge. Damian wanted to hit him again; his eyes flicked to Dusty, but she shook her head, mouthing, *I will ground you.*

He lowered his arm, finished the meat he held, and washed his hands.

"Do I have to go with?" Duke mumbled into the fridge.

"Yes, you and your brother have to go together. Damian was born with instinct; you need to learn it." Dusty hugged her youngest and ruffled his hair.

"I don't get it. We are twins. He is like five minutes older than me—"

"Yeah, and I got all the good stuff. You got the leftovers." Damian flicked his brother's ear.

"Stop it!" Duke smacked away Damian's hand.

"Good grief! Do you want to go to your separate corners like you did when you were five?"

"No, Mom," they sang together.

———————

All three dressed in black with tight-fitting clothing, with their hoodies pulled over their heads. The silver moon shone through the trees and lit up their back yard—the nature reserve Dusty's family owned and had lived in for centuries.

They shared the reserve with a handful of *normal* families.

Dusty dug her left foot into the ground, looked up at her two sons and beamed with pride. "Are you ready?" Both gave her the thumbs up, and all three kicked off into the night. The boys darted to the left of her and disappeared. She manoeuvered to the right, near the river that ran through the reserve. Many animals drank there; if she could catch a buck or a kudu, they could eat for a few days. Dusty's ears prickled as she caught sight of an owl on a branch that kept its eyes on her as she passed it.

After yesterday's rain, the air still smelled of damp sand and wood in the aftermath of today's sultry afternoon. A stench of dung caught her attention as she ran over debris from fallen tree branches. The wind must have blown stronger this side of the reserve.

Being in her natural habitat, she was hyperaware of everything and every creature around her. Something shifted within. Her body wanted to change completely, but it was no longer necessary; she only changed those parts that were needed—her claws, her soft padded feet, and sharp teeth. Her kind were naturally more powerful by being a werewolf by birth, and not one due to an attack. Therefore, they could shift quickly or only the parts that were necessary.

Not too far away, Dusty heard a heart pumping blood throughout an animal's body while hers slowed down. The padding on her feet muffled the sounds of her footsteps. Her animal scent tricking the wild game into thinking there was no danger. A buck browsed a distance away, and she crept towards it. She jumped from one fallen tree trunk to the next until she drew near. A hare sat between fallen branches, looked up at Dusty with its black eyes. She lifted her sharp claws at it and it scurried away.

The buck didn't know she was there yet; it blissfully ate dinner. She steadied herself, and with a powerful leap, she pounced onto it. Dusty went straight for the neck and bit down. With the prey secured, her sharp teeth pierced the hide with ease. Blood flowed into her mouth and down her chin, leaving a sweet metallic taste in her mouth. She forced her teeth deeper into the animal's neck, and its heart slowed down. The buck collapsed, but she gripped tighter, biting down harder. The animal gave one final jolt, and its heart stopped. The buck went limp. She released it and wiped her mouth on her sleeve. Her catch was quick and pain-free.

Dusty threw the buck's body over her shoulder as if it weighs nothing and jogged home.

As Dusty reached their house, she heard a throaty yowl for a few seconds and then it stopped. No animal came close to any of the houses, especially not theirs, so this animal had to be quite a distance, and possibly in pain. It didn't make another sound, and Dusty didn't think of it again.

Duke watched Damian take the lead; his body naturally stronger and larger than his. They may look similar, but the differences were distinct; they shared the same shade of sandy blond hair, Damian preferred it short while Duke kept it longer. Damian's build was muscular and strong, a few inches taller than his twin. While Duke's physique was that of a swimmer's—he wasn't lanky, but more of a medium build and like normal guys their age.

Damian leaped from one low tree branch to another,

then landed firmly on his feet without breaking a sweat. Duke tried to follow in his big brother's footsteps but couldn't leap as high as him and settled on a branch lower than where Damian was. Damian held up his hand, meaning Duke mustn't move. Duke followed Damian's line of sight to see what made him stop. Up ahead was a warthog. Damian glanced at Duke and pointed for him to go around the animal. They would trap it from both sides. Slow and steady. Duke went around until he was as close to the warthog as possible so that if it tried to run away, Duke could catch it. But it was Damian who would go in for the kill.

Damian vaulted from the darkness over tree stumps onto their prey. Duke watched Damian bite into it but turned away before he could see more. There were some things he preferred not seeing because once it's seen he couldn't unsee it. Duke's head swooshed and his knees couldn't keep him up any longer.

Duke jumped—half fell—off the branch and crumpled to the wet ground. He kept his head down, strained his eyes to focus on insects crawling near his hand, to blades of grass they were carrying, then the hole they disappeared into.

When the smell of blood invaded his nostrils, he closed his eyes, waiting for it to happen. The animal cried, and Duke couldn't keep his food down anymore. Tears streamed down his face, and he wiped away the vomit before his big brother could see it.

Pain stabbed his chest for the life of the animal his brother took away. But he knew it's only meat, food for their family, meat for them to live. But knowing that it was once a living creature brought sadness, and his heart ached.

Dusty threw her kill onto the chopping table and butchered the animal into manageable sizes. She heard the crunching of leaves and voices outside followed by heavy footsteps coming up to the door. Damian entered the shed and handed her the freshly killed warthog.

"Where is your brother?"

"He's outside. He doesn't want to come in here. And he doesn't know I heard him vomit again."

"Ah, no! Let me finish up here first before I come inside the house. I will speak to him later."

She gutted then skinned both animals; their hides still in excellent condition, and she could sell them once she finished treating them. Their meat hung inside the walk-in fridge. Her family had more than enough meat to last them for the next five days. As she closed the fridge, something stopped her from shutting the door properly. She pulled the door open again, looked inside near the latch but couldn't find the cause. Dusty re-entered the fridge. Standing on the tips of her toes, she felt the top of the door frame, nothing. She glanced on the floor and froze. There were five little holes about half a centimeter in diameter each, with rough edges in the floor. One of the boys must have dropped the meat tenderizer, and when they pulled it free, it left those five little holes. When she opened the door, she must have caught them again and lifted the edges. The edges pushed against the door frame, making it stick.

Dusty imagined something laying its eggs inside and wanting her to touch the exterior of the holes so it could strike. She saw a cluster of eyes staring back at her from the darkness of the little holes. She blinked and stared at it again. Now there's nothing. It's just five little holes. But her fear was playing tricks on her. Unless there really was a family of little creatures living inside trying to make their way up, to make their way to her?

Sweat beaded on her forehead, and even though the interior was cold, her face and hands were hot. She anchored her legs to the fridge's floor. She glanced up at the chopping table. If only she could move and get to the table, to where the knife was; she could use the handle end to flatten the edges of the holes to close them. Chilled air escaped her lungs, and clouds of her breath surrounded her.

One foot at a time, she reached the fridge's door. The shed's door opened and closed.

"Who's there?" Dusty saw his shoes first then glanced up to see Malcolm standing with his hands on his hips and his chest out—the hero she needed right now. She whimpered.

Malcolm grabbed her by her shoulders and yanked her out. "You looked stuck, honey." He chuckled.

Dusty bumped against the chopping table and wiped tears from her eyes. "Th-the hole." Dusty exhaled. "There are five tiny holes at the bottom there." She pointed to the area near the door frame.

Malcolm crouched down, felt over the holes with his fingers. "Easy." He fetched the knife and with the butt he hammered the edges flat and covered the holes. He closed the door, and it latched tightly.

———————

The feast on the dining table could easily feed a small wedding reception. They ate the same amount of food every night, and only once a day, only at home and always together as a family.

The boys usually snacked during the day, but that's only because they needed to. They were sixteen and still growing. They had lots of skin to fill and muscle to build.

Every evening they waited for Malcolm to arrive home from work. The boys helped their mother set the table and prepared the meal. Usually, there was always some type of organ in a bowl for them to share: raw kidneys, a heart, liver or even lungs. Their main dish was usually ten to twelve rare steaks. Sometimes they included thinly sliced rare steaks marinating in soy sauce—all animal meat and all caught during the week.

Dusty included a green salad and another, either baked potato or a potato salad. They didn't eat bread, dough or any other kind of staple food; it's terrible for their guts. The rare steaks and organs were mainly for three of them. Duke had his own special plate of food made up of meat that had been seasoned and hung to dry for at least four or five days, and he ate the green salad and potato dish—he was the *vegetarian* in the family.

Duke was also the only one who helped his mother make the dessert—chocolate pudding with ice cream frozen in the intestines of a wild animal. They usually preferred the blood to be hot or warm, but now and then it's a delicacy to have it iced and mixed in with something sweet.

With the table set and the kitchen clean, Dusty closed the dishwasher door and switched it on. Malcolm was in his chair clasping a beer and watching a sports channel she didn't recognize.

"When are you going to hunt with us again?" Dusty asked.

"I'm too tired when I get home from work," he said, still watching the screen. "Besides, you don't need me. Damian is good enough for both of us."

"It would be nice for you to go out with us once in a while, Malcolm." She grabbed his free hand. He glanced up at her—his eyes shifted and changed from their usual warm brown color to gold, then back to brown. One side of his cheek dimpled in.

"Maybe next weekend?" she asked.

"Maybe."

She left him to watch his sport. Her skin crawled when he slurped his beer. He could be such an animal sometimes. Her lips curled upward as she considered that; he was one.

Duke was silent during dinner; he barely finished his meat, and she had to put both salad bowls, untouched, back in the fridge. She wanted to talk to him after dinner, but he darted upstairs so quickly she didn't have the chance. She wanted to let him know everything would turn out fine. His nausea would sort itself out. Their type always did.

Dusty traversed upstairs and rapped lightly on Duke's bedroom door. He didn't respond. She knocked harder.

"Enter!" he yelled.

"Hey, baby."

"Please, stop calling me that," Duke growled from behind his trigonometry book.

She would always call him her baby, no matter how old he was. "Getting ahead before the term starts?"

"Uh-huh."

"It will be okay." With two fingers she pressed down lightly on the book to see his face. He tried to lift it back up, but she was stronger than him. "We all do things in our own way, and at our own pace. You just need to figure out yours."

"Like Damian?"

"No, you are nothing like Damian. You are gentler and kinder." She sat beside him on his bed. "You just need to find a way to manage how you feel when you hunt with Damian and the kill. We differ greatly from the rest, and I wish there were more like us, but they are spread out across the world."

"It's the blood." He threw the book on the floor and sat up. "I can't handle the sight of it. If I see it, I become queasy."

"What part of it makes you queasy?"

"The smell of it, the metallic taste. It's not so much the kill but the cries—" He swallowed the words he wanted to say, hugged his stomach.

"Give yourself time and try to think of the animal as food and nothing else. We don't hunt for sport, we hunt to eat. If we don't eat, we die. Besides, the two of you only started hunting on your own this year. The more you hunt, the easier it will become."

"Is that what Dr. Byrd tells you?"

"All the time." She ruffled his hair.

"But, why? Why do we even have a weakness? I thought we're supposed to be these big powerful creatures, yet we all have some sort of hang-up?"

"It's what keeps us human." She winked darkly.

Dusty exited Duke's room and checked in on Damian. His bedroom was dark, and she waited for her eyes to adjust to the blackness. She couldn't see him. The window opposite the door was open. She approached the opening and stuck her head out. The cool autumn breeze chilled her skin and felt her smile reach her eyes until something slimy climbed up her leg. Glancing down at the slug, Dusty tweezed it with her fingers and threw it out the window.

Hairs stood on the back of her neck. She turned around to face the room. She focused on the black shadow in the corner. Her ears tingled and she slowed her heart beat so she could hear his. Keeping her eyes in the shadow's direction, she heard the *da-dum* of a pulse. The first life she gave. The frequency of the *da-dum* sped up and the shadow jumped. She leaped into the air; they collided and crashed. Dusty pinned Damian to the floor with her knee on his broad chest.

"You are not that quick yet, my boy." Dusty softly patted his cheek.

Damian laughed, tapped out, and she got off him.

"You are getting stronger, Damian." She said with pride. "But promise me one thing?" she waited for him to acknowledge. "That you will look after your brother. Be patient with him."

Damian sat up. "Sure Mom, but he needs to learn fast. I can't babysit him forever."

"Just for now. Until the two of you are full grown." She switched on his bedroom light. "And clean your room. You aren't a pig." She laughed down the hallway and into her bathroom.

Dusty rested her hands on the wall as the scalding water caressed her entire body. She stared down at the make-shift cover she placed over the drain. It's not as frightening as the original drain with all the beady eyes staring back at her. She toed the improvised cover, ensuring it's still firmly in place. Steam filled the bathroom once she closed the taps, climbed out and wrapped the towel around her body.

Malcolm entered their bedroom, and threw his shoes on

the floor with a grunt. Dusty opened their ensuite bathroom door to see her husband lying on the bed. With a swagger of her hips, she sauntered over to him but pulled her nose up and away from the smell. She patted his enormous stomach, and he jolted up, shaking the bed.

"You need to lose this gut of yours, sweetie. You used to be a beast of an animal and now you're just lard." She giggled, then tapped his gut again, so it wobbled.

"Ya, ya. I will get to it." He rubbed his belly in a circular motion, then placed his arms above his head. "I will get to it."

"You should stop working so much, maybe spend a little more time with us." She grabbed her pajamas from the drawer and pulled them on.

"Ah, not again, Dusty. Please." Malcolm sat up and massaged his face with both hands. "I like what I do. The kids are all grown, and they hunt with you when you get home from work. When you work. And things have changed. It's unnecessary for me to hunt with you anymore. We basically have the entire reserve to ourselves now."

"That's not the point, Malcolm. You must want to spend time with us once in a while. Lately, all you do when you get home is eat, drink beer and watch sports. Your sons still need you, no matter how old they are. A boy always needs his dad. Both are going through their changes and they need you." Dusty threw her towel in the laundry basket and sat beside him.

"Do you know Duke can't stand the sight of blood? He throws up every time. And Damian, he's brave and strong, but awful scared of heights. He can never go to the highest treetop."

Malcolm's mouth opened slightly, and he pressed his fingers against his temples. "I didn't know."

"You need to fix that. You need to be present."

"I will." Malcolm rubbed Dusty's back, kissed her cheek. "And what does Dusty need?" He nuzzled her neck and a low guttural growl escaped his mouth.

She pressed her head against his, then stood. "Only when things change." She left him on the edge of the bed and climbed under the covers.

"Ah!" he complained and stomped into the bathroom.

Dusty shivered, pulling the duvet over her shoulders. The cool air was icy on her cheek. She pulled the covers past her ears. The house was freezing, and it wasn't even winter yet. Her eyes fluttered open. Darkness streamed in from the outside. She reached for Malcolm, but his side of the bed was cold and empty.

Sitting up, she focused on her surroundings. The faucet dripped slowly (Malcolm needed to fix it), an owl hooting, but there was no familiar sound coming from the house. Duke's light breathing and mumbling were silent. Damian's deep-chested exhales weren't echoing throughout the house.

Silence.

Sweat beaded down Dusty's forehead and she climbed out of bed, grabbed her gown from the nearby hook and slipped it on before she opened her cupboard to retrieve her boots. Dusty waited and listened. Still no sound from the house. She descended the stairs two steps at a time, stopped at the bottom and listened for any of the men in her life, but they weren't inside or anywhere near the house. The front door stood wide open. She was sure it was closed and locked. She didn't think anyone would enter, but they always kept their doors closed and locked.

Her hearing was excellent, yet she didn't hear them leave—was it the deep sleep of late?

Why did they leave the house without waking her?

Did Malcolm hear something and didn't want to disturb her?

Questions swarmed her mind, but she had no answers.

Once outside she stared at the empty house with the trees surrounding her, and Dusty felt out of sorts. She pulled her gown tighter around her body and wrapped her arms around her waist—her heart beat quickened not for the thrill of it but for the panic that had slipped down her spine and into her chest cavity. Somehow the history with the Cravens seeped into her mind and what they were capable of doing—to finish the fight they had started with her sons —but they would never do something this drastic, could they? Why not take her as well?

The hairs on the back of her neck stood on end as she directed her attention toward the outside world. The trees and darkness of the night beyond their house, she listened to everything. They had to be somewhere in the reserve and she would find them.

Dusty exhaled and dropped her shoulders. Her heart-beat slowed down, and she steadied her breathing. In the far distance, a faint yowl sounded followed by a growl; she shifted her body in that direction and sprinted. Dusty ran until she reached the far edge of the cliff where the water flowed over and into one of the four ponds. Buzzing caught her attention. A hive, alive with bees; multiple honeycombs dripped with honey. Dusty froze, rigid at the sight of the waxy structure, each cavity dark and crawling with bees. She had to fight her fear and move away from it to find her family. As much as she hated to admit it, she remembered what Dr. Byrd had told her during one of their many sessions, about the mindful breathing and the relaxation techniques—she would beat this fear. She closed her eyes and breathed in the cool air. The smell of rain lingered, then she exhaled. Slowly she opened her eyes and with one step at a time, she maneuvered around the tree until the honeycombs were no longer in view.

Hissing and growling sounded to her far right, and she ran in that direction. The disturbance was coming from the far side of the reserve, an area where they rarely hunted.

Dusty reached her destination only to discover a wild cat stuck in a trap—the cause of the racket. Surrounding the wild cat were her boys; they were trying to free it. A smile stretched across her face and wiped away a tear. They hadn't noticed her arrival, so when she touched the back of Malcolm's shoulder he jumped.

"We need to put a bell on you." Malcolm grabbed her hand. "Mama cat's stuck, and her babies are waiting for her over there." He pointed to rocks where eight eyes glowed in the dark.

"How long have you been here?"

"Not long," Malcolm kissed her cheek. "I couldn't sleep. I kept thinking about what you said, so I woke the boys after midnight for some hunting. We heard a mama-cat cry and came straight over."

"Who set the trap?" Dusty asked.

"I think it's the Cravens, Mom," Damian answered as he approached the cat. "You know how much they enjoy canned hunting; this is just another way for them to get their rocks off."

"Yeah, I remember." Dusty looked at Malcolm with wide eyes.

"You two must be careful of them if you see any of

them out here." Malcolm draped an arm around Dusty's shoulders.

Duke scruffed the cat gently while Damian loosened the trap from around her paw. There was some damage to her skin, but she would heal. She seemed too tired to fight or bite Duke and allowed him to pick her up and drop her near her kittens. They watched as mom and babies scuttled into the night.

"Well done, son." Malcolm gave Duke a hug.

Damian and Duke bumped fists.

"You're a natural, Duke. That mama cat didn't even hiss at you."

"It felt good." He beamed at the compliments.

Dusty watched her sons and wanted to burst with pride, not only for Duke but also for Damian—her two boys worked so well together.

Malcolm came beside Dusty, wrapped his meaty arms around her waist and brought her in for a kiss.

"Is this better?"

"Yes,"—Dusty stroked his chest, — "much better."

The receptionist was clicking her pen nervously when Dusty walked in. She stopped the clicking and said. "Dusty, you are a little early for your appointment, dear." The receptionist looked at the clock and then at her computer. "By thirty minutes."

"It's okay, I don't mind waiting." Dusty sat on the chair with the best view of the entire office. She could see the receptionist, the door to Dr. Byrd's room, and the entrance. She kept herself busy by reading last month's fashion magazines.

The red light above the door dimmed and the green light illuminated, followed by a click. The receptionist stood and knocked on the door before opening it; she said something to Dr. Byrd and then motioned for Dusty to enter.

Dusty entered the room where Dr. Byrd was already sitting, waiting for her.

"Early again, Dusty." Dr. Byrd looked at her from above the rims of his glasses. He pushed the frames back onto his nose. "Please, sit."

"You know me, doc, always early."

Dusty sat opposite him in the comfortable one-seater. She made a mental note that they should get one for the house. She shifted in the seat then settled down, tapping her fingers on the armrests.

Dr. Byrd scribbled something.

"What?" she blurted and folded her arms across her chest.

"Relax, Dusty. How have you been?"

Dusty wanted to tell him she was dying to get back to the hospital, to her patients. She loved working in the emergency room where fresh blood fell at her feet and she could lick her fingers without getting caught.

But she had to be here.

She also wanted to tell him it worried her the Cravens might cause trouble again. It wasn't her fault their daughters gave off a scent which raised havoc in her boys.

All she said was, "I'm better." She cocked her head to the side and plastered on a smile.

"And…"

"And, just better." She shrugged.

"We only have a few sessions left before I have to send them my evaluation. You have come so far from when you first arrived." Dr. Byrd's mustache curled up; it looked like a hairy caterpillar slept on his upper lip. "Like I always say, the more you face your fear, the easier it will become. One step at a time."

Dusty's stomach gurgled, and she was sure he heard it. Her kind only ate animal meat, but sometimes she had urges to eat annoying people. It didn't have to be a full moon for them to hunt; they hunted any time they felt like it.

Unfortunately, for obvious reasons, the pack prohibited them from eating humans. However, she had had enough of Dr. Byrd's weekly meetings. All he told her she was like so many others who shared her phobia.

But she wasn't.

She was nothing like *other* people.

That's the trouble with psychologists—they liked to compare. They coddled and told their patients they mustn't feel bad, and that there were others out there just like her.

She white knuckled the armrest and sensed a shift in Dr. Byrd's demeanor. She stretched her fingers and drew in a deep breath.

Dr. Byrd watched her intently and spoke in a soft tone about facing her fears and working hard so she could reap the rewards. Whatever.

She had to be here.

The hospital needed to know she was okay before she could return to work, that the holes weren't an issue anymore.

It was one slip-up. The bullet hole in the man's head had dark-seeded tendencies and had wanted to hurt her. It was an accident. She had pulled out the bullet, and he coded.

She was facing her fears every day, now.

Tried.

So, now she needed to play along. If she could go back to work during the next few weeks she would let Dr. Byrd live. But he looked so soft and tender today, and he smelled so juicy.

Would he be missed?

Did he have a family? He didn't have a ring on his finger or photos on his desk.

Her stomach sounded again, and he definitely heard it.

"Are you hungry?"

"I'm famished." She licked her lips.

TWO

New Girl

Two days ago

Tara and Melinda stood across from each other, with the autopsy table between them. The corpse lay on top with a white sheet covering him up to his waist; he was nude above the waist. Melinda moved her hands over the body in a circular motion and started chanting.

"Are you sure it's even him, Mom?"

"Yes, I'm sure."

"It's not even her fault. Why do we have to do this to her?" Tara pointed to the corpse when she said *this*.

"She is her father's child, and he made his choice—he left me and took his pregnant woman away from here all those years ago. But he has come back, he has returned to me, Tara. I need to teach him a lesson and make sure his offspring understands where she fits in. Sins of the parent are the sins of the child. Don't forget that."

Tara stared at her mother and rolled her eyes. That was not what she wanted to hear right now. That meant whatever her mother did throughout her life was now Tara's sin as well. That's not really fair, was it? Tara's head hurt just thinking about what her mother had done throughout her life.

"We aren't going to hurt her, just scare her. Right?"

Melinda opened her eyes and nodded at her daughter. "It's just a little scare, nothing permanent. And I will deal with her dad later."

"Oh, all right." Tara sighed. Not wanting to upset her mom, she lifted her hands and moved them in unison with her mother's.

They chanted the words together, over and over.

Tara felt her mother's power engulf her like tiny pinpricks over her entire body. Her arms pebbled from the power splashing across her skin. She wasn't as powerful as her mom yet and still had a lot to learn, but her mother taught her something new every day.

A warm wind smacked Tara in the face, and she almost lost her balance. She kept her feet further apart to stay upright while maintaining the circular motion of her hands in time with her mother's. The warm wind surrounded them like a baby tornado, moving faster and faster around them and the autopsy table. Tara's arms burned all the way up to her shoulders, and she wanted to drop them. Melinda's green eyes turned golden and met Tara's. Sweat beaded down Tara's face, but she wouldn't wipe it away, not yet. She needed to keep up.

Melinda smiled.

The body on the table shook. Black blood pooled over his stomach.

The dead man exhaled a black cloud of chalk and it floated into his opened skull and into the little pieces of brain matter.

TODAY

Jess's pulse thumped loudly in her ears. The constant *lub-DUB, lub-DUB, lub-DUB*. Her throat was dry. She swallowed hard, but it didn't help. She had to swallow a couple of times before her throat felt clear again. Not sure if it was the creaking of the door as they entered the basement or the darkness that surrounded them, but she wanted to turn back and go up the stairs. Tara held her hand, and Jess couldn't decide whether it's for comfort or to make sure she didn't run away.

Jess never thought of it before, but now that she was standing on a step on her way down into the basement: it's not only in the movies that mortuaries were in the basement and in old, creaking houses.

Jess held her breath a second too long, then opened her mouth so she could exhale and inhale. At least the air was cool and fresh.

Tara flicked on the light switch, and the passage was bright, blinding Jess for a second. The walls were the color of eggshells, with three old paintings hanging on them. Tara was still holding Jess's hand.

"Come on, scaredy-cat." Tara glanced over her shoulder at Jess and smiled.

"I'm not scared." Jess pouted.

She was scared, but Tara didn't need to know. Jess straightened her shoulders, lifted her head and could now see over Tara's head. They turned a corner where two doors were situated on their left, with another straight ahead. There was one more door, a glass sliding door to the right. Jess wasn't sure she wanted to enter that one.

25

"Here we have Mom's office." Tara pointed to the first door on the left but didn't open it.

"The bathroom," Tara opened the door. "It has the best shower in the entire house."

The room's color was disco pink, straight from the eighties.

"I know it's bright. We are tackling this room over the weekend, and I can't wait."

Tara led Jess to the door that was straight ahead.

"The coffin room," Tara opened the door.

A stale wood smell tickled Jess's nose, and fine dust particles floated in the sliver of sunlight cascading through the tiny window.

"We're working on that too. We want to knock out the window over there." Tara pointed to the right-hand side of the room. "It will open up onto the delivery ramp from the autopsy room." Tara closed the door, and they headed toward the last room. This was the largest of them all. The smell of disinfectants was prominent.

Jess pulled her hand free from Tara, wiped her hands on her jeans and stood steadfast in the doorway, too frightened to enter. A light flickered overhead and she could've sworn she saw something move in the corner. Or her mind was playing tricks on her. Tara had been speaking about this the whole day at school. Listening to Tara talk about what her mom did, Jess visualized the mortuary differently. It's a lot scarier in real life when all the elements were put together; the smell of dried blood, a rotting corpse in the fridge, disinfectant that burned her nostrils, and the icy air that kept the room cool or the dust from the coffins.

Jess looked from the corner to the middle of the room where the autopsy table was. Someone was lying on it.

"It's really okay, Jess. He's dead."

"But I can see the body on the table."

"Have you ever seen a dead person before?"

"No, is there blood?" She hadn't seen her mom when she died. But now that she was older she wanted to see what a dead person looked like but at the same time not. Reluctantly, Jess stepped closer. Her heart thumped and her clothing clung to her body.

Tara approached the table and stood on the other side of the corpse, near his head.

"I want to show you something."

"Uh-uh," Jess shook her head.

"Suit yourself." Tara tugged on the corpse and pulled something off his head, lifting it up. It's the man's skull.

"Oh, my! What are you doing, Tara?" Jess couldn't move. Nausea brewed in the pit of her stomach. There were red chunks of something on the inside of his skull. "Is that his brain?"

Tara bared her teeth in a grin. "Cool, isn't it?"

Jess's breakfast rose in the back of her throat and stopped breathing. She leaned one hand against an empty table to keep from falling over. The walls closed in and the body in front of her grew bigger and closer. It sat up, its black orbs for eyes glistened in the shadows and its mouth opened revealing sharp teeth. It reached out to grab her, its arms stretching to find her. When she blinked, the body was on the table and unmoving.

"Are you okay?" Tara lifted the hand holding the skull up toward Jess as if she wanted to reach out and grab her, to try steady her. With the momentum of the motion, a chunk of the brain matter flew through the air and hit Jess on her cheek.

Jess shrieked loudly, "Get it off. Get it off. Get it off." She clawed for the soft chunk of brain on her face and scraped parts of it off. Tears stung her face, her stomach lurched and vomited on the floor and her shoes.

"Oh, my gosh! Oh, my gosh! Oh, my gosh! Are you okay?" Tara shrilled, ran to the metal cupboard and pulled out a towel and wet wipes. She pulled five wet wipes out at a time and wiped Jess's face and hands, then gave her the towel to dry her face. Then she fetched the bucket and mop and started cleaning the mess off the floor. Jess gagged but stopped herself from ruining the floor again. Jess ran to the basin and started washing her face and eyes, rinsing her mouth out with water.

"I thought I was going to die, Tara. What the fark man? You didn't have to fling that shit at me."

"I didn't mean to, Jess. It was an accident. I didn't know the chunks were fresh and loose."

Jess gagged over the basin again, but there was nothing left to spit out. Her entire body shuddered as she replayed the chunk of brain landing on her cheek repeatedly in her mind; it would take a while for her to unsee it. She wiped away tears and had a burning desire to leave and go home, but the thought of everyone laughing at her at school stopped her.

"Do you still want to sleep over?" Tara asked and giggled.

"Ha-ha, you're very funny," Jess answered from the bathroom. After her little incident, they went upstairs so she could shower. Her stomach was still in knots and empty.

"My mom is making a salad for you. I hope that's all right?"

"Salad is fine, thanks." Jess opened the door to see Tara sitting on her bed painting her toenails black.

"Sorry I am laughing, but it was funny."

Jess smiled, but it didn't reach her eyes. "Just don't do it again, please. My stomach can't handle it."

––––––––––––

"I hope you two are hungry?" Tara's mom asked Jess as they sat down for dinner.

Jess eyeballed Tara, "Yes. Thank you, Mrs. Bailey."

"Please call me Melinda, Jess. I am not that old, yet." She smirked at her. "So, Tara tells me you are vegetarian. I hope you like the salad."

"It's perfect, thank you. And please don't go out of your way to make food specifically for me. I am happy to eat the non-meaty food you prepare." Jess forked a tomato and ate it.

"So, Jess, tell me. Where did you and your father move from? Tara only gave me half a story."

"Well, my folks actually grew up here, maybe you knew them? They married and moved away before I was born. When my mom died last year, my dad decided to come back. That way I'm closer to my nan and she can help out while he works."

"Who is your dad and your nan?" Melinda asked while slicing through her banger and scooped mash onto it.

Jess was so used to calling her grandmother nan, she forgot her real name sometimes. She paused for a second, thinking. "Mary Hollow, and my dad is Nick Winter."

"Oh yes, we know her and your dad's name rings a bell," Melinda chimed. "Your nan is a sweet old lady. And, your dad, what does he do now that he's back in town?"

Jess caught a look between Tara and Melinda, followed by a change behind Melinda's eyes. When she had first met

Melinda, her eyes were green, but now they were almost yellow or golden, with a hint of green—they were strikingly beautiful. She ignored their exchange and continued talking. "He works for the mayor, some office-type stuff. Politics bore me, so I really can't say what exactly he does."

Jess emptied her plate while bubbling noises came from her stomach; it sounded so loud she looked up to see whether Tara and Melinda heard. Jess wasn't paying attention to what they are saying to each other, instead—all she thought of was food. It's impossible that she was still hungry as she just ate.

The salad Melinda had made would usually keep her full for at least a couple of hours, but not today.

Jess eyed the leftover mash in the dish on the table; shrugging, she scooped it up and dished it onto her plate.

Tara and Melinda didn't say a word.

That evening, Tara and Jess watched scary movies and ate butter-soaked popcorn. No matter how much Jess ate, her stomach wanted more. They fell asleep before the second movie ended.

Throughout the night, Jess tossed and turned, uncomfortable no matter which way she lay. She dreamed of the basement stairs: the dark, creaky staircase that led down into the cold mouth of death. The walls were pale green and expanded and contracted; alive and breathing. Something told her to search, to look, even though she didn't know what it was she was looking for. She opened the office door first. Melinda's space was tidy; all her files were stacked neatly on top of one another. On the wall behind the desk was a picture of Melinda and Tara. In the picture they looked like sisters with their matching brown bob hair, green eyes, slender faces, and athletic builds. To the left of them was a setting sun, the glare complimenting their complexions. They seemed happy without a care in the world. A filing cabinet to the right moved like the green walls. She approached and pulled on each of the handles until the middle drawer opened. Inside was a ring that used to belong to her mother—her wedding ring. She picked it up, and stuffed it in her pocket. Something else was calling her. She exited the office and entered the eighties-looking pink bathroom. The shower curtain was drawn. The shadow that stood on the other side of the curtain moved, and Jess froze mid-step. Slowly, she reached for the curtain even though she was trying as hard as she could to bring her arm down and away from it. As if her hand was possessed with a mind of its own, she grabbed the curtain and yanked it open. It's only a towel hanging over the shower head; with nothing else inside.

She opened the third door where the coffins were kept. These were stacked on shelves, four against each of the three walls. All slightly open except for one. When it opened she reached to see inside. Jess flinched and stepped back from the billowing cloud of dust. When it settled, she leaned over and peered inside. The coffin was empty apart from an old jewelry box she used to have as a kid. Jess opened it and the ballerina sprung straight and twirled while music played. She removed the ring from her pocket and placed it inside the jewelry box and took it with her.

Jess slid the fourth door open and shivered as she entered, hugging herself. The corpse was still on the table; only this time his skull was on his abdomen. Red stuff oozed out from the skull and dripped over the body. She heard her mother calling out to her, telling her to leave. To run home. Not to pick it up.

No longer in control, she reached for the skull. It wanted her to pick it up. It called out to her. The foreign voices forcing her fingers to come into contact with the cold bone. The instant she touched it, the body on the table sat up. Jess jumped backward. The skull fell from its abdomen and shattered on the floor like glass-shards scattering everywhere, just missing her feet. The corpse lifted its arm; it wanted to touch her. The thing grabbed her right arm as she turned to leave and burned its fingers into her skin.

Jess screamed in pain, with Tara shaking her awake.

"Jess wake up," Tara repeated then let go once Jess opened her eyes. "You were screaming in your sleep."

"I'm awake. You can get off me now."

Jess sat up and wiped sweat from her forehead. Her stomach ached and a terrible pain shot from somewhere around her abdomen and into her chest. She winced.

"Ow!" Jess grabbed her chest, jumped from the bed and ran to the bathroom. She hunched over the basin, spitting and coughing up what she thought was bile. When she opened her eyes and examined what she brought up, she saw black tar-like-goo with wriggly worms slithering in it. Jess gagged, then glanced in the mirror above the basin. Her skin was pale, almost translucent; she could see all her veins like a map in a book. There was more white around her eyes as she stared in disbelief at her reflection, then back at the worms. Cold sweat ran down her back and she closed her eyes, wishing away the black goo and worms. Jess opened her eyes, and the basin was still black and moving. She turned both taps on and washed it down the drain, careful not to touch any of it.

She felt as though she was dying. Hoping she didn't have

a dreaded disease and was on her way to sleep in a coffin forever. At least she didn't have to go far.

She knew something was wrong; she wasn't feeling panicked or screaming at the top of her lungs. Knowing there should be fear, anxiety, or something, but there was nothing.

Numb was all she felt.

A strange warm breeze twirled around her body like a cat licking milk out of a hand, the sandpaper tongue causing goosebumps on her skin. Her shoulders sagged like the weight of the black goo and worms was keeping her tense and anxious. She stared at her face in the mirror again and the road map of veins was gone, leaving her skin flawless and colorful once again. In the mirror, her green eyes smiled back at her and her mouth curved upwards. Without knowing why or how she understood; but it would be okay.

Calm was what she felt.

Everything would be all right.

Jess opened the bathroom door to find Tara sitting on her bed and staring at her with wide green eyes.

"I'm starving," Jess said.

In the kitchen, Tara placed the milk and cereal on the counter, but Jess was hungry for something *else*.

And she was H-U-N-G-R-Y. No cereal in the world would satisfy her hunger.

There had to be something more *filling* she could find.

Jess opened the fridge door and spied each shelf. She saw what she wanted, what she needed, and removed the container from the fridge filled with cubed raw meat. This was something that would ordinarily make her gag, make her turn up her nose and run away, raw or cooked. Yet today, the smell of it drew her in. The smell was like freshly bloomed roses waiting to be turned into perfume. The smell of rain just before the drops fell. The rich batter poured into the tin and baked into a cake. It's a smell she couldn't quite place yet triggered something deep within her: the need for rich raw meat.

A creature waiting inside of her, clawing its way out in need of meat.

Raw meat.

Jess dug in with her hand, brought a cube to her mouth and chewed loudly. There was no gagging, no nausea, no disgust. There was only calm and relief as she felt the cold chewed meat slide down her throat and feed the creature within.

Tara's mouth hung open. "Jess, that meat is for tomorrow? You aren't supposed to eat it, and you don't even eat meat." Her voice was pitched higher than usual, but it didn't bother Jess.

"I'm sorry, I really am. I know this looks terrible and my behavior is awful, but I can't help it, I can't stop myself. I have never felt so ravenous before." Jess licked her fingers, caught the juice running down her arm with a lick of her tongue. "I need to eat it. All of it." Jess bit into another cube and maroon liquid dripped down her chin. She wiped away the blood drops with the back of her hand. Her heart thundered in her ears and her forehead tingled where the sweat beaded. The power of the raw meat coursed through her veins, and it burned. Like fire spreading throughout a house, it spread through her veins from her mouth to her fingertips, all the way down to her toes. It was magical yet felt normal, like she was supposed to feel like this. She felt as though she could walk through walls and hoped it wasn't permanent.

Tara's eyes widen.

Jess smiled at her and shrugged. "I can't get enough of it. It makes me feel invincible."

Melinda entered the kitchen and gasped. "Oh, my! I thought you said she doesn't eat meat, Tara."

"She doesn't. I didn't know this would happen. She vomited again this morning and then she said she was hungry."

"What do you mean by again?"

"Um."

Melinda turned to face Tara. "Um?"

"We went downstairs yesterday, and I picked up that man's sawn-off skull. When I lifted it, some of his brains splattered across Jess's face."

"Did you clean her face properly with disinfectant?"

"We wiped her face."

Melinda ran downstairs and returned quickly carrying a tub.

"What is it, Mom?" Tara stepped out of the way and stood on the other side of the kitchen island.

"While I was busy with that man's autopsy, I discovered he was contaminated with something. Apparently, they found him in the lake near the old mill. There, where they used to make the guns. That's why I removed the top part of his skull, to send a sample in for testing." Melinda unscrewed the cap. "You need to be careful, Tara. It could have landed on you."

Melinda and Tara exchanged a knowing look. That same golden color flared in Melinda's eyes, and then in Tara's. Jess opened her mouth to say something, but then

Melinda scooped chunks of the cream and said. "Where did it land on your face?"

Jess pointed to the spot. Melinda's smile reached her eyes and then she smeared the cream onto her face where she pointed. Jess expected it to burn, instead her skin tingled. The cream cooled the area, and Jess hadn't realized her face was so hot before the cream. The disinfectant smell wasn't as strong as the room downstairs, but it was pungent enough. The coolness spread down her neck, easing the tension in her shoulders, and it moved further south, into her stomach like an instant release. The cold sensation traveled through her hips and down into her legs and toes, ending with a pinprick.

Her trembling hands steadied.

Her heartbeat evened out.

Her hunger was satisfied.

She glanced down at the bowl, at the thick, curdling liquid and chunky pieces of meat. The kitchen blurred and her head ached. She placed the bowl on the table and stepped backward. Jess looked up at Tara and her mother. She wasn't sure of what she saw, but it looked as though both their eyes were completely golden now, and their smiles showed teeth. She stepped backward, tripped over her heel and crashed to the floor. Her body slammed hard against the table, and her head struck the corner. Bright sparks swam across her vision and her eyelids closed. Jess's head was too heavy to lift, and all she remembered hearing was Tara asking her mom if she was happy now.

Eighties songs played: *Beat it* ended, and *Sweet Child O' Mine* began. Jess was lying on her back. She cleared her throat, and it was dry; burned when she swallowed. A metallic taste filled her mouth, and her head throbbed. She lifted her hand and felt the back of her head. Luckily it's only a bump, not serious and there was no blood.

Blood!

Jess opened her eyes. She was in Tara's room. She remembered the raw meat she ate for breakfast. Ugh! The cream Tara's mom had smeared on her face. Double ugh! The dead man's skull and the brain matter. A shiver ran down her spine. It all felt real yet dream-like?

Her stomach turned.

Jess sat up and the room spun for a moment; she was alone with the door ajar and music coming from the lounge. Tara's giggle was followed by a loud thump on the floor. Jess stood and descended the stairs—Tara and Melinda were dancing. They stopped once they noticed her.

"How are you feeling, Jess?" Tara walked over and hugged her. "We were so worried."

"What happened?"

"You fainted after I messed the brain matter on your face yesterday and you slept straight through."

"Fainted?" Jess rubbed her temples, her head was sensitive. "I had such a weird dream. It felt so real, though."

"Would you like me to call your dad to come fetch you early?"

"Yes, please. If you don't mind?" Jess looked at Tara; she didn't want to offend her friend by leaving early.

"No, not at all." Tara wrapped her arms around Jess for a hug.

There was a faint smell of disinfectant surrounding Tara, and the dream Jess had flashed before her eyes. Her knees weakened, but she kept upright. There was something awfully familiar about this, the way they stood and glared at her, waiting for her to say or do something. It's almost as if their eyes have a story to tell, but she couldn't figure it out. A golden color flickered in Tara's eyes when she turned to face Jess; she remembered how their eyes glowed, and she wanted to retreat but then remembered her tumble. She noticed the table, and that nothing had broken. She felt confused.

Melinda entered the kitchen to phone her father, then returned and said. "He said he should be here in about twenty minutes."

"Thank you." Jess forced a smile. She just wanted to go home. If only her dad could get here sooner, but she couldn't wait twenty long minutes with them.

Jess would rather wait in Tara's room where she took her time packing her things. She only ran down when she heard her dad's car, his Ford's engine unmistakable. When the doorbell rang she thanked and hugged Tara and Melinda.

In her embrace with Melinda, Melinda leaned closer and whispered in her ear, "I made your mother eat meat once." As she said *meat*, she pulled away from Jess to stare her in the eye and winked.

Frosty air trickled over Jess's body as Melinda spoke, and before she could say anything, her dad was standing in the doorway. When he saw them, saw Melinda, his eyes showed more white, and his mouth parted. An *uh* sound escaped his lips as recognition flickered in her father's eyes. It was obvious he knew Melinda, but he didn't say anything. If she didn't know her dad so well, his silence and expression made her think he was angry, but she knew it was pain. Why would he feel pain if he knew Melinda? How did he know her?

Then, what Melinda had said about her mother registered. She must have known her mother when they were young and still lived here. What Melinda did to her—she said she did to her mother as well. A ball of twisted butterflies formed in the pit of her stomach, and she had to leave now. She didn't want to know more about what had happened all those years ago, and she didn't want to spend any more time near Melinda or Tara.

Jess ran to her dad who stood in the doorway and hugged him tightly. She pressed her head to his chest so she can hear his heartbeat and felt his warmth. She was safe again.

As they were about to leave, Melinda stalked to them, near her father and said, "I didn't think you would ever return, Nicky." She said his name with a hiss under her breath. "You left me and ran away with your precious bride before I could tell you about *your* daughter." Melinda placed an arm around Tara's shoulders, bringing her in for an embrace.

Daughter?

Was Tara his daughter?

Jess looked into their green eyes: so green, the color of spring leaves. The same color as Jess's and her mom's eyes.

Jess could feel her dad tense in her arms, and she didn't want to let go of him, not just yet. And all he seemed able to do was just stand there and say nothing. Shock would do that.

"Don't worry, Nicky. I won't hurt her again." She lifted her hand to touch Jess's cheek, but her dad pulled her out of reach. "You know I would never, ever truly hurt my niece."

Jess coughed and choked on Melinda's words: she was her mother's sister, her aunt; Tara was her cousin.

Jess stared up at her dad for confirmation, but he

seemed too afraid to look at her or to blink—when he did those watery eyes would spill tears of bottled secrets.

He finally found his tongue, "Come Jess, it's not worth it, let's get out of here."

Jess studied her dad and saw anger and hardness she'd never seen before.

He glowered at Melinda and added, "That's enough Melinda, we have a truce, and I won't hesitate telling your family what you did."

Melinda lifted her hands in mocking surrender, "Then be gone, Nicky." The door slammed in their faces.

Jess's dad wiped his eyes dry. "I didn't know it was her, pumpkin. I was told she moved away. I would never have left you here if I'd known."

"It's okay, Dad. It's over."

"There is much I need to tell you, secrets we promised to never tell you. But after today, after learning Melinda is still here and has a daughter, *my* daughter. You must never see either of them again, and never alone. Melinda is powerful and very dangerous."

"Okay."

"Let's go to Nan—she has to know what her daughter did."

THREE

Damned Soul

They were outside again.

Robert placed his tools on the table beside his seat and stood, peered out the window but far away from the light. His fence was a distance from his house, but he could still hear *them*. They laughed, teased each other, threw a ball and ran around. The frequent bouts of laughter and shrills pierced his inner ears and sent shock waves throughout his body.

He hated children.

They were messy, noisy and painfully dependent on adults. Robert paced in his lounge; but out of the sun's reach like dusk fingers clawing at him. He was meant to be sleeping, but he had been around for so long that he only needed a few hours of sleep during the day to function properly.

Should he extend his fence further or have another word with their parents? Dull-witted parents made dimwit children. He couldn't reason with any of them.

He couldn't even hear the howling outside or the stridulating sounds from crickets or hoots. They drowned the calming white noise out by screaming laughter. He grunted and sat down again. He needed to keep busy and not think of the creatures out there.

The glass case beside him was dusty. He wiped it down with a special cloth from Italy. He only used the best for *her*. His stomach tightened and pained. He squinted at the calendar that hung on the wall across from him and saw it had been two days already. Pain shot down his spine and weakness threatened his body. He had been so busy fixing her glass case he forgot to eat. He never forgot to eat. He glanced at her glass case with admiration and smiled. That was why; there was a crack in her glass case and he had to repair it the moment the new glass panel arrived. He couldn't leave the case unfinished just so he could feast.

Robert flinched when a knock sounded at his door. He pulled the door open so hard the little person on the other side jumped back in fright. Big brown eyes stared back at him.

"What do you want?" Robert demanded from the safety of the dark shadows.

"Sorry, Mr. Clemente, we kicked our ball over your fence, and I need to fetch it."

"Well, what are you waiting for? Go get it and go away."

"It's near Rufus." The boy stepped back and pointed to the sleeping dog near the side of the house.

"Don't make your problems mine. I don't have time for this." Robert slammed the door shut.

Robert stalked to his spare bedroom and yelled at the drawn blinds near the window, "Rufus. Move, boy."

The sleepy bloodhound dragged his ears and chains to the front door, allowing the boy to fetch his ball.

When the boy retreated to the fence, Rufus stood lazily and went back to his sleeping spot.

Robert frowned.

They were too comfortable around him. That kid jumped his fence like he lived here. He placed his hands on his hips and paced again. He needed to change the facade the families had of him and had to show them what he was capable of doing. For years he had left the families who lived near him alone. He always sourced food far away, but maybe he needed to change that. But first the sun had to set.

Robert rocked in his chair and held his favorite Gaetano Giulio Zumbo picture. A wooden frame surrounded it with a model of the *Damned Soul* in the middle—the suffering sculptor was made out of wax, had protruding veins and bulging eyes with flames surrounding his face. He was desperately screaming for help while stuck in the depths of Hell. Robert understood what Gaetano must have been feeling when he made it. It felt all too real for him staring down at the wax figure; *so tired, so lonely, so hungry.* When Robert first lived in Italy, Gaetano had given him the frame before he died in 1701. That's when Robert fell in love with the art of wax, the warm sensation of molding anything he desired and sculpted it with his cold, lifeless hands. He gently wiped dust out the corner of the wooden frame until he was satisfied and hung it on the wall again near the front door. He walked past the glass case that rested in the middle of his living room and stroked it gently.

Venus was lying on her back with her head tilted slightly backward and her legs bent a little at the knees. The silk sheet beneath her was the same royal blue as her eyes. Her shapely figure forever crystalized with wax until the end of time, until the end with him. The smiling photograph of them hanging alongside the *Damned Soul* on the wall didn't do her justice. She was more beautiful in real life. More beautiful lying quietly in her glass case, forever.

The golden light glimmering through a gap in the lounge blinds informed him it was almost time. He should get ready. He grabbed the body bag from his closet cupboard and flicked on the oven switch to warm the hard wax. Tonight, he would feast then mold what he wanted to keep. He trailed his fingers across her glass case one last time before heading out.

The sun had disappeared, and darkness surrounded him and his house and the forest in which he lived. Yelling could be heard on his left and right. He gripped the body bag and jumped over his fence in one swift motion, landing with steady feet on the ground. On the outskirts of his fence, there were a few houses within the reserve the others called home. He was the first to stake his land, hence he had the largest stand of all. When the others asked to live here, he had allowed it; he had agreed to share. But there could be no more new families allowed on the land with them. Everybody lived off the land. But some parents would leave the reserve to work. And everybody had left him alone—until recently. The children started playing closer and closer to his fence. And today, one climbed over. The nerve!

There were twenty homes in the small village so it would be easy to find out who the child was and who he belonged to. Robert strolled along the path until he reached the water well in the center of the village. He rang the little bell that was bricked at the top of the water well wall. A man from each of the homes scurried out, with a few hushed sounds and shushing from others. Dennis, the leader of the village, approached Robert with his hand outstretched. Robert stared down at the dirty palm and then at his face.

"Robert." Dennis realized Robert wasn't going to shake his hand and dropped it to his side. "Is something the matter?"

"Yes, Dennis, there is something seriously wrong."

Dennis's eyes widened when he saw the bag over Robert's shoulder.

"Anything we can do to make it better?" By then all the men had joined them by the well and glanced among each other; some shrugged, but all utterly confused and scared as to Robert's presence in the village.

"Your children know no boundaries."

A hushed whisper near the back caught Robert's attention, and he scowled at the two men. They stopped talking.

"How long have I allowed you to stay here with me?"

"About twenty years," Dennis responded quickly with the others echoing him.

"Now that's a long time, isn't it?" All the heads nodded in agreement. "What was the condition for you all to live here?"

A man beside Dennis wiped his brow. Robert could smell his stench and pulled up his nose.

When nobody answered, Robert glared at Dennis, who promptly said, "That we are to leave you alone, and you will leave us unharmed." Dennis looked to his fellow neighbors for confirmation.

"That's right, yet your snot-faced children think it's fine to play near my fence, and today one of them jumped over to retrieve a ball."

Gasps sounded at the back, followed by mumbling.

"How can we make this right?" Dennis asked with a tremble in his voice.

"Give me that child."

"What does he look like, Robert?"

"Brown eyes and a scar across his left eyebrow."

"No!" shouted a father on Robert's right.

"Come here," Robert called after the man. "Your son had no qualms jumping over my fence. To disturb my place of rest. Why are your children not taught, given chores or things to do around the house?"

"I beg your forgiveness, please don't take my only child away." The man fell to his knees and cried. It's too pitiful for Robert to look at.

"What is your name?"

"Wayne."

"Wayne, what is your son's name?"

"Charlie."

"Why do you only have one child?"

"His mother died during childbirth."

Robert nodded; he remembered one woman had died about fourteen years ago. Her screams echoed in the trees. He considered this.

"All right, Wayne. I won't kill him immediately, but I do still want him."

"Why?"

"Would you rather I drained him in front of you?"

Wayne cried. "Please don't take him away from me."

They were all warned when they moved here. He left them alone if they left him alone. Why did they not listen? If they couldn't keep their children in line, he would do it for them. Robert needed to teach them all a lesson. He reached for Wayne and pulled him closer. Robert placed his hand on the man's shoulder, moved his collar out of the way to reveal a clean neck. He could see Wayne's heartbeat at the spot he liked best; the soft skin where fresh warm blood gave life. Robert pushed Wayne's face to one side, closed the gap and bit down hard. His sharp teeth pierced tender flesh and slashed through veins, warm blood nourishing him and filling him—satisfying his need, his hunger. He drained Wayne and dropped him when done. The crowd surrounding him stepped backward, afraid they would be next. Cries cut through the evening silence. Robert wanted to laugh. Why were men crying? What was wrong with this generation? They were all so ... sensitive.

Robert wiped blood from his mouth and regarded them. "Anyone else wish to defy me?"

"No, Robert," Dennis said with his hands in the air, a sign of subordination. He was proving himself to be a useful leader. "Please, nobody else."

"Fine. But I still want the boy. Bring him to me within the hour." Robert dropped the bag on Wayne's body and turned to walk away.

There were whispers and cries as Robert floated away from them. Before he was too far away, he yelled over his shoulder, "And bring me Wayne's body." A few of the men gasped.

Dennis yelled back, "Okay."

Charlie knocked on the wooden door: holding a shaky fist in his other hand, swallowed hard and fought back tears. There were delicate engravings etched out along all four sides of the ancient door. He glanced at the bloodhound sleeping on the right and glad he wasn't stalking him—there weren't many dogs in the village and those they did have were all afraid of the bloodhound. He glanced over his shoulder and waved timidly at Dennis.

Footsteps neared, then the door yanked open with Robert staring down at him. The full moon shone brightly around them, and Robert's eyes were no longer a gloomy gray from this afternoon but silver; his piercing gaze burning into Charlie's head. Charlie flinched and remembered to look away and focused on Robert's pale skin instead. Robert looked the same age as his dad, mid-thirties, but he knew Robert was much, much older than that—by a few hundred years. Nobody seemed to know his true age, and nobody wanted to ask. The hairs on the back of Charlie's neck rose, and sweat ran down the middle of his back. He wasn't this scared this afternoon when he had first knocked on Robert's door. Was it the darkness and he simply never noticed how scary Robert was? Or was Robert pulling some kind of power over him to make him scared?

"Is it Charles or Charlie?" Robert's voice was deep and authoritative yet alluring—a voice so velvet-smooth and charming it could make you share all your secrets.

Charlie glanced up, but not directly into his eyes—more at his lips.

"Charles. But everyone calls me Charlie."

"I am not everyone." Robert arched an eyebrow.

Charlie sniffed and wiped his nose with the back of his hand.

"Didn't anyone teach you how to blow your nose?"

Charlie nodded.

Of course, he knew how to blow his nose; he just didn't have a tissue on his person.

"Well, don't just stand there. Come in."

Charlie hesitated, glanced over his shoulder again, but Dennis was gone. He stalled for a second then stepped inside, then Robert brushed past him to go outside. From the bottom of the stairs Robert picked up Charlie's father's body—that was safely tucked into the black body bag—as if he was as light as a feather, Robert opened the basement doors and threw him down the steps like trash. Charlie swallowed hard and sniffed again. His hands bunched into fists and his arms strained. That was his father that Robert threw like that. He wanted to blame Robert; it was his fault his father was dead—he had killed him, sucked his life away. But he couldn't completely blame Robert, since this was his own fault. He entered the vampire's land without batting an eye. He was too comfortable. He stared at Robert who was now returning to the front door and his chest thumped with anger. Would he be able to fight Robert? He had never hit anyone before but looking at Robert's evil eyes then glancing down again, all he wanted to do was pound his fists into the vampire's face for taking away his father.

Robert walked his fingers across Charlie's shoulders. "Don't even think about it, boy. I will snap you like a twig."

With the warning, Charlie was forced to back down. He closed his eyes and his shoulders sagged, trying to release all the tension he was holding inside. He wouldn't be able to fight Robert and live.

"How do you know what I want to do?"

"I've been around a lot of angry boys to know the difference between them wanting to fight me or being scared. The look on your face tells me there is much fight in you—like an angry fire trying to escape. One thing you need to understand, I will not hesitate."

The power coming off the vampire felt like tiny insects scratching all over Charlie's skin; he crossed his arms and started rubbing them. Maybe it would soothe the burning sensation.

"Yes, sir," Charlie averted his eyes and stared at his feet, and entered the house.

The interior of the house smelled like dust and old things. Only a dim light illuminated the lounge. Charlie squinted to see where the furniture was so he didn't walk into anything. Robert came in behind him, pushing Charlie out of the way so he could close the door.

"Well, Charles, did Dennis explain things to you? About why you are here?"

"Because I came into your yard this afternoon, and because of that you killed my father." Charlie looked solemnly up at Robert. "What are you going to do with me?"

Charlie fought back the tears, opened his hands and wiped them down his thighs, leaving dampness. The memory of Robert draining his father was still fresh in Charlie's mind. What would happen to their house now that it was empty? Who would live there now? Would they leave it untouched until Robert allowed him to come back, or would Hansel and Mary-Anne move in now that they were engaged? Was he about to die by the same hands that took his father or would he grow old? A million and one questions flew through his mind while he stared up into Robert's face, not his eyes. He didn't know if those eyes would force him to do things he didn't want to do and he shivered.

Robert interrupted his thoughts when he approached an oven that stood near the far wall. There was a large pot with something warm inside and steam rising. Robert switched off the oven and flipped on another light. Charlie adjusted his eyes to the new light and felt his eyes widen, his jaw slacking. Body parts made of wax on shelves near the oven: a heart, a pair of lungs, and even a kidney. They were all encased in glass tombs. There was a reclining chair with a table, ancient and leathery. The next wall had pictures; Robert with a beautiful woman who had long dark hair;

they looked very happy. A bench sat underneath a window that faced the front of the house. Charlie turned to his left where a wax man screamed from a wooden frame near to the door. Charlie covered his mouth as he whimpered; studying the room further and blinked away tears. It was a room made up of nightmares. He said a silent prayer to keep him safe. There was a door leading out to somewhere; perhaps the kitchen. In the middle of the lounge was a large glass coffin with another wax figure laying inside; it was the woman from the pictures with Robert. Charlie looked from the picture to the wax figure and back again.

"She died very young."

Charlie met Robert's gaze for a split second before looking back at her. "She's beautiful."

"That she was." Robert stepped closer to Charlie and to her, placed his bony hand gently on the case. "I love her very much."

"Why didn't you turn her?" Charlie bit his lip, regretting the words the moment he said them, and stepped away from Robert.

"I couldn't torment her like that. I've lived an immortal life, and I was tired by the time I'd met her. I did not want to ruin her innocence by keeping her like a possession."

Robert was offering much information, and Charlie would rather keep him talking. He didn't know what Robert wanted to do with him, but talking was always better.

"How did you meet?" Charlie stepped closer, feeling relaxed and a little comfortable.

Robert lunged at him, hissing. A few things happen in those seconds. Charlie stepped back again but not far enough, Robert's hands moved too quickly for Charlie to see him coming, and Robert's long fingers curled around his throat and squeezed.

"You are too comfortable near me, boy, and I fear nothing will ever curb you of your curiosity. At least you are pretty enough that I can look at you as often as I want, even with that scar."

Robert touched the scar with his free hand while the other squeezed Charlie's throat, the bones cracking beneath his strength.

Stars sparkled in front of Charlie's eyes and the darkness surrounded and swallowed him whole.

Robert placed the second pot of hot wax on the table beside Charlie's still body. Next to him was a row of large vintage metal syringes, modified to include a thick-enough needle for the wax yet thin enough to enter a vein. The two puncture wounds on Charlie's neck where he had drained enough blood to keep him still but not enough to kill him would suffice; a beating heart worked best for even distribution. Charlie's wrists were bound in front of him and set more to his left-hand side. There was a wooden block under Charlie's head, raising it slightly and to the left. He was half on his side, half on his back with a block keeping his back in place. His knees were bent and close to his chest with his feet bound at his ankles.

He looked like a sleeping angel praying to his God but worshiping Robert.

Robert could feel his smile reach his eyes, wiping his hands on his apron and moved hair out of Charlie's face. Robert leaned closer to stare at Charlie's face; his pale skin so pure and delicate like a flower yet to bloom, and he smelled faintly of vanilla and soap.

With Robert's touch, he would preserve the young boy for eternity.

They were in the kitchen. Since Robert didn't use the room to cook, instead he used the space to make his wax sculptures. There were wax statues made up of wild animals; a fox, a squirrel, and even a lizard. There were also limbs, organs, a fetus and two human heads—male; all neatly placed on shelves surrounding the room.

The table with Charlie's body on was in the middle of the kitchen making it easy for Robert to grab a tool, a scalpel, a syringe or more wax easily and still be able to move around.

Robert filled one of the large syringes from one of the pots with wax the color of blood and aimed carefully at the large vein in Charlie's neck; there was a slight pulse thumping the vein outward. Robert entered the vein with the sharp needle at a twenty-five-degree angle and pushed the warm wax in. The blood did the work and beat the wax through the veins and into his heart and throughout his body. Robert filled the syringe again and repeated the process over and over until all the veins were full and his heart had stopped.

Robert grabbed the scalpel and sliced from sternum to his groin. He opened Charlie's chest cavity cleanly and parted the skin; with the syringe, he injected the pink wax into each of the organs until it filled every space. Robert repeated the process over and over until every empty area on Charlie's body was full of wax and slowly setting. As it cooled, Robert started on the skin; inserted more wax throughout and then with his hands, he scooped sizable chunks of cooling wax and covered the skin—molding, shaping and setting it in place—the way he liked it.

Robert stood back and tilted his head to the side, admiring his beautiful handiwork.

Apart from Venus, Charlie's body was near perfection. Robert unclipped the lock on the wheels of the table and wheeled Charlie's body into the next room where he would cool completely and set.

———————

After feeding on an animal or two, Robert sat in his chair, rocking gently while he listened to the birds, the wind blowing through the trees, and nothing else.

There were no children laughing, no children playing, no children anywhere near him.

There was only the sound of his rocking chair, the animals outside, and his thoughts.

Robert leaned his head against the back of the chair and smiled.

vinci-books.com/monsterfeat

Three monsters. Three nightmares. One terrifying collection.

From the deadly song of mermaids luring Vikings to their doom, to a cursed Mayan temple demanding fresh sacrifices, to a Scottish family's horrifying duty to feed a colossal kaiju—*Monster Features* brings legends to life in three chilling tales. Enter if you dare.

About the Author

Multi-genre author writing twisted endings...

N Gray is a USA Today Bestselling Author who lives in Cape Town, South Africa, with her daughter and adopted cat named Miss Beans.

During the day, she's an analyst and provider profiler for a medical insurance company. At night, she types on her curved keyboard, creating fictional characters some may love and others you want to kill yourself.

She writes in four genres: urban fantasy, thriller, horror, and paranormal romance.

She now writes under Natalie Michaels for her new thrillers and SD Syns for her new horrors.

Acknowledgments

Dear Reader

I write in as many genres as I love reading in. There are so many stories swarming inside my head that I could never just choose one.

Horrors are my guilty pleasures. I love writing short stories filled with dark humor and the occult with a twist ending.

Urban fantasy and Paranormal Romance are where I love to spend my time and I have so many books planned that I don't have enough time (*but I'll get there*).

And lastly, my thrillers. Who doesn't love sitting on the edge of their seat while reading about what goes on inside the antagonists mind. Well, I love writing about them.

You can view all my books on my website. They come in ebook format as well as paperback, and most are in hard cover.

Until the next book, stay safe and keep reading.